Pebble® Plus

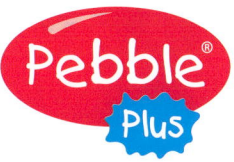

Places in Our Community

Our Law Enforcement Center

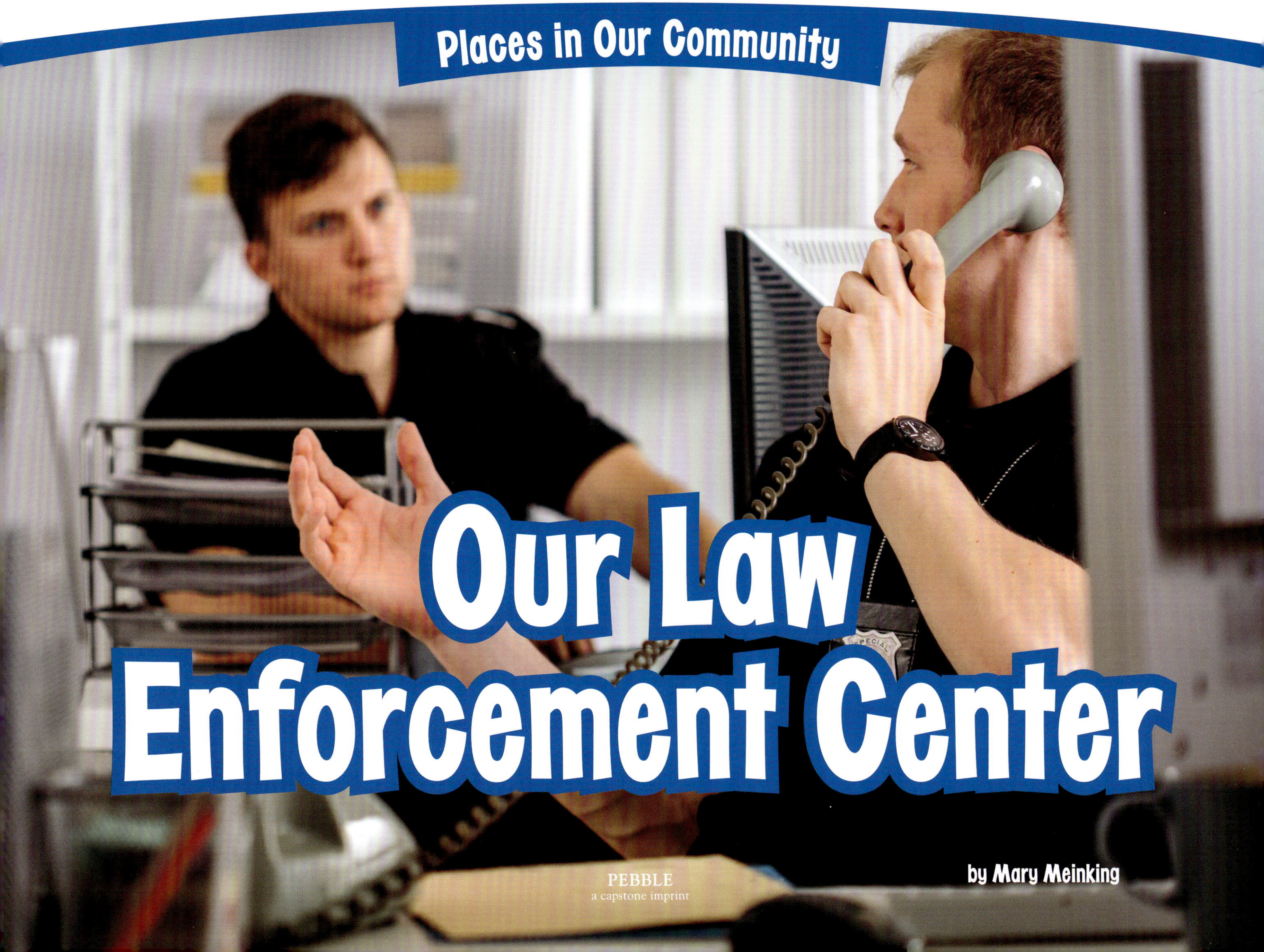

by Mary Meinking

PEBBLE
a capstone imprint

Pebble Plus is published by Pebble, an imprint of Capstone.
1710 Roe Crest Drive, North Mankato, Minnesota 56003
www.capstonepub.com

Copyright © 2020 by Capstone. All rights reserved. No part of this publication may be reproduced in whole or in part, or stored in a retrieval system, or transmitted in any form or by any means, electronic, mechanical, photocopying, recording, or otherwise, without written permission of the publisher.

Library of Congress Cataloging-in-Publication Data is available on the Library of Congress website.
ISBN 978-1-9771-1261-3 (library binding)
ISBN 978-1-9771-1768-7 (paperback)
ISBN 978-1-9771-1267-5 (eBook PDF)

Editorial Credits
Editor: Mari Schuh; Designers: Kay Fraser and Ashlee Suker; Media Researcher: Eric Gohl; Production Specialist: Katy LaVigne

Photo Credits
Alamy: David R. Frazier Photolibrary, Inc., 9, imageBROKER, 21; Getty Images: Darrin Klimek, 13; iStockphoto: RichLegg, 11, 17; Newscom: MCT/Mark Randall, 19; Shutterstock: Alexxndr, 2 (notebooks), Andrey_Kuzmin, 23, Barbol, 2 (background), Betelgejze, 3, Drop of Light, 7, Elisanth, back cover, 4, 6, 8, 10, 12, 14, 16, 18, 20, John Roman Images, cover, LightField Studios, 5, Photographee.eu, 1, PRESSLAB, 15, Sean Locke Photography, 24, vmargineanu, 22

Note to Parents and Teachers

The Places in Our Community set supports national social studies standards related to people, places, and environments. This book describes and illustrates a law enforcement center and the people who work there. The images support early readers in understanding the text. The repetition of words and phrases helps early readers learn new words. This book also introduces early readers to subject-specific vocabulary words, which are defined in the Glossary section. Early readers may need assistance to read some words and to use the Table of Contents, Glossary, Read More, Internet Sites, Critical Thinking Questions, and Index sections of the book.

All internet sites appearing in back matter were available and accurate when this book was sent to press.

Printed and bound in China.
002493

Table of Contents

Let's Visit a Law Enforcement Center 4

Who Works at a Law Enforcement Center? 6

What Happens at a Law Enforcement Center? 12

Law Enforcement Centers are Busy Places 18

Glossary 22
Read More 23
Internet Sites 23
Critical Thinking Questions 24
Index 24

Let's Visit a Law Enforcement Center

Have you ever wondered where police officers and sheriffs work? They work at law enforcement centers. Let's find out more!

Who Works at a Law Enforcement Center?

Police officers and sheriffs keep people in the community safe. They make sure everyone obeys laws.

Jailers watch over people who are in jail. Jailers also take people who are in jail to a courtroom.

Judges work in a law enforcement center too. They sit in a courtroom. They listen to cases and study the facts.

What Happens at a Law Enforcement Center?

Police officers or sheriffs meet

at the law enforcement center.

They plan their day. Then they

go out to patrol streets.

They may drive cars or ride bikes.

13

If someone breaks a law, that person is taken to a law enforcement center. An officer snaps a photo and gets fingerprints.

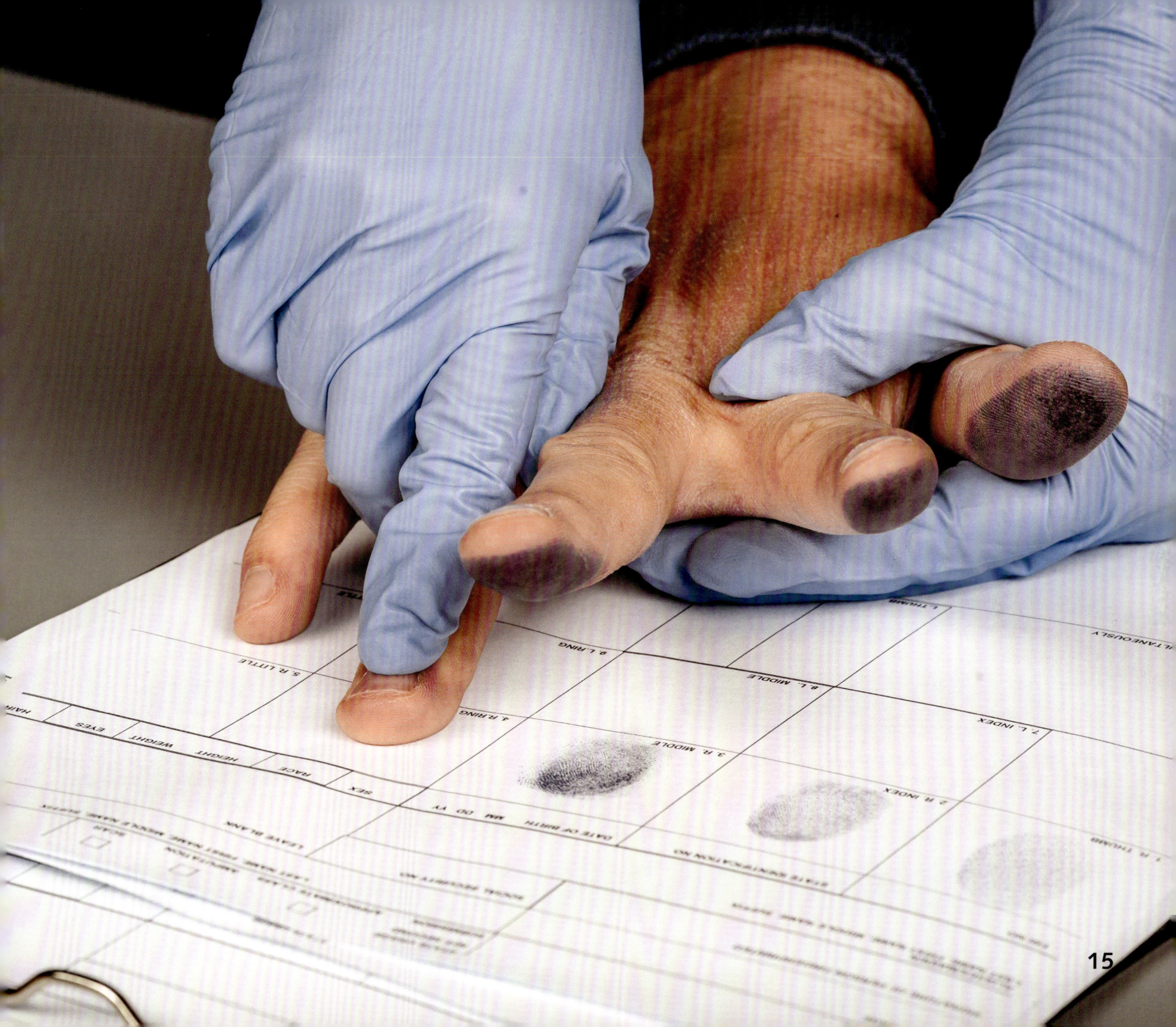

The jailer takes someone to the courtroom. The person tells her story. Officers also share what happened. A jury or judge decides if a law was broken.

Law Enforcement Centers are Busy Places

People call 911 when they need help. Their calls go to a dispatcher. She sends officers, firemen, or rescue people to help.

Law enforcement centers are busy places. Everyone works as a team. They work to keep people safe.

Glossary

arrest—to stop and hold someone for doing something against the law

case—a crime the police investigate

courtroom—a place where court cases are heard

dispatcher—a person who answers 911 calls and sends rescue workers

jailer—the person who watches over people who are in jail

judge—a person who makes decisions on cases in court

jury—a group of people at a trial that decides if someone is guilty of a crime

law—a rule set by a town, state or country

patrol—to protect and watch an area

sheriff—the person in charge of enforcing the law in a county or town

Read More

Donner, Erica. *Police Station*. Minneapolis: Jump!, Inc., 2018.

Murphy, Patricia. *The Police Station*. North Mankato, MN: Capstone Press, 2018.

Murray, Julie. *The Police Station*. Minneapolis: Abdo Kids, 2017.

Internet Sites

Easy Science for Kids: Police Dogs Saving Lives.
https://easyscienceforkids.com/all-about-police-dogs/

National Child Safety Council: Materials for Kids
https://nationalchildsafetycouncil.org/materials/materials-by-age/kids

Community Club: Police Officer
http://teacher.scholastic.com/commclub/officer/

Critical Thinking Questions

1. List two people who work at a law enforcement center.
2. In what ways do police officers or sheriffs keep people safe?
3. What phone number do people call in an emergency?

Index

911, 18

cases, 10
courtrooms, 10, 16

dispatchers, 18

fingerprints, 14

jailers, 8, 16
jails, 8
judges, 8, 10, 16
juries, 16

laws, 6, 14, 16

patrolling streets, 12
police officers, 4, 6, 12, 16, 18

sheriffs, 4, 6, 12